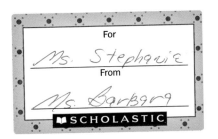

For

Ms. Stephanie

From

Ms. Barbara

■SCHOLASTIC

FROGGY GETS A DOGGY

FROGGY GETS A DOGGY

by JONATHAN LONDON

illustrated by FRANK REMKIEWICZ

SCHOLASTIC INC.

For Asta, Keeper, Xavy, Toto, Eli, Kailen, Helene, Evie, Iris, Doran, Pat, and sweet Maureen
—J.L.
For Austin, Jack, Sarah, Andreas, and Loki
—F.R.

ISBN 978-0-545-77518-2

12 11 10 9 8 7 6 5 4 3 2 1   14 15 16 17 18 19/0

Printed in the U.S.A.   40

First Scholastic printing, September 2014

It was night.
Froggy woke up
and looked out the window.
"The moon! The moon!" sang Froggy.
"It looks like the tail of a happy
doggy!"
(Froggy knew what he wanted
more than anything in the world—
a dog!)

FRROOGGYY!

called his mother next morning.
"Wha-a-a-t?"
"Time to get up, dear!
We're going to the animal shelter!"

"Yippee!" Froggy hopped out of bed and got dressed—*zip! zoop! zup! zut! zut! zut! zat!* . . .

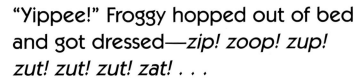

then flopped to the kitchen—
flop flop flop.
"I think we'll get a bunny," said Mom.
"I don't want a bunny!" cried Froggy.
"I want a doggy!"

"But you can't have a dog, dear.
Dogs are too messy."
"I'll clean up after it!" said Froggy.
And he ate his bowl of cereal and
flies—*munch crunch munch*—
(and left quite a mess).

Pollywogilina started smacking
the table with her spoon, singing,
"Dog-g-y-y! Dog-g-y-y!"
and Froggy joined in—
"Dog-g-y-y! Dog-g-y-y!"

"Quiet!" said Mom.
"Or no pet at all!"

Froggy flopped back—*flop flop flop.*
"Look at the bunny!" said Mom.
"Isn't she cute!"

"Dog-g-y-y! Dog-g-y-y!" sang Polly.
And Froggy joined in—
"Dog-g-y-y! Dog-g-y-y!"

"Quiet!" said Mom.
"Or no pet at all!"

"Now what about this darling baby gator?" said Mom.

"No!" said Froggy and Polly.
"Or these mice? Mice are nice!"

But Froggy ran off to see the dogs—
flop flop flop—
and was about to stick his hand
in a cage.

FRROOGGYY!

called Mom.
"Wha-a-a-a-t?"
"Stay here! Stay near!
AND DON'T STICK YOUR
HAND IN A CAGE!"

But when Mom got to Froggy . . .
the cutest little doggy in the world
had stuck her nose out of the cage
and was licking Froggy's hand—*slurp
slurp sluuuuurp!*

"Please, Mom!" said Froggy.
"Just look at her eyes!"

Mom looked—

and the little doggy looked back.
And her sweet chocolate brown eyes
melted Mom's heart.

"I think I'll just name her Doggy!" said Froggy.
"Dog-g-y-y! Dog-g-y-y!" sang Polly.

When Froggy got home,
he couldn't wait to play with Doggy.
"First," said Mom,
"you have to put on her new collar
and fill her water bowl
and show Doggy her bed."
"I *know!*" said Froggy.

Froggy put on Doggy's collar—
znap!

And filled her water bowl—
glug glug glug!

And fluffed up her bed—
ploof!

"Now," said Froggy, "I'm going out to play with Doggy!"

"First," said Mom,
"you have to put on her leash
and take her for a walk
and teach her to come and sit and wait!"
"I *know!*" said Froggy.

"And," said Mom, "don't forget to take your pooper scooper with you, and clean up after her!"

So Froggy put on Doggy's leash—*znap!*
And took her for a walk—*sniff sniff sniff!*

And when they got back,
he tried to teach her to sit up and beg . . .
roll over . . . and shake hands.

Then along came Frogilina.
"Hi, Froggy! What a cute little doggy!"
"And she's smart!" said Froggy.
"Watch her fetch the stick!
Fetch!" said Froggy.

But Doggy knocked over
the badminton net . . .
and the birdbath . . .
and sprinted into the house.

DOGGGGYYY!

called Froggy.
Arf! said Doggy.
"Wait! Come! FETCH THE STICK!"

But when Doggy raced back out . . . she had Mom's UNDERWEAR instead!

"Oops!" cried Froggy,
looking more red in the
face than green.
"Sit?"

Frogilina laughed
and said, "Good Doggy!"

That night, Froggy put Doggy into her bed. But Doggy . . .

wanted to sleep with Froggy.
And she snored!—
snuffle-snuffle-wheeeeeezzze—
all night long.

But just before the sun rose . . .
Doggy licked Froggy's face—
sluuuuuuuurp!—

and scratched at the door—
scritch scritch scritch!
(She had to go out—bad!)

Mom held out a toy shovel, and said, "Don't forget your pooper scooper, Froggy!"

"POOPER SCOOPER!" squealed Polly,
and everybody laughed—
even Doggy. *Arf! Arf!*